Published by Modern Publishing,
a Division of Unisystems, Inc.

Copyright © 1986 Victoria House Publishing Ltd.

Designed for Modern Publishing by Victoria
House Publishing Ltd., 4–5 Lower Borough Walls,
Bath, England

® —Honey Bear Books is a trademark owned by
Honey Bear Productions Inc., and is registered in the
U.S. patent and trademark office.

Printed in Belgium

THE HUNGRY HIPPO

Written by Stewart Cowley
Illustrated by Colin Petty

MODERN PUBLISHING
A Division of Unisystems, Inc.
New York, New York 10022

When Potamus Hippo woke up one day,
He felt in a wonderful mood.
He went to the cupboard for peanut butter and jelly,
For that was his favorite food.

But oh dear, the cupboard was bare,
Of peanut butter and jelly there was none.
He searched and explored, but all he could find
Were some nuts and a very stale bun.

"Oh darn it!" he grumped as he pulled on his hat,
"I have got to find *something* to eat."
He stomped down the stairs and stomped out the door,
Though he was usually quite light on his feet.

Now hippos are big and hippos are plump,
Their bodies are heavy and lumpy.
The ground always shakes if they stomp when they walk
And hippos stomp when they're grumpy.

"Please, Mr. Hippo!" cried the Skyscraper Bird,
"You're shaking my nest to the ground."
But Potamus just kept stomping along
With no peanut butter or jelly to be found.

All through the forest, the animals clung
To their very best china and glass.
Even the loud Pandemonium Beast
Had to cover his ears when Potamus passed.

At last young Potamus came to the store
Where he usually bought his supplies,
He gasped when he saw there was no peanut butter or jelly,
He could hardly believe his own eyes!

"Oh no!" he bellowed. "What am I to do?"
And he threw his hat to the ground.
He crossly stomped on it terribly hard
Until it was flat and not round.

"What can we do?" said the Woolly Gnu
At the meeting place down by the creek.
"He's doing more damage in one afternoon
Than an earthquake can do in a week!"

"Perhaps we could give him some carrot soup,
Or some sweetcorn with butter and salt?"
"Why don't we give him some figs?" asked Jimmy Giraffe,
"Washed down with a big chocolate malt."

"That's no good," said the Lion, "but I've got an idea.
We'll *make* peanut butter, jelly and toast!
Let's gather up corn to make plenty of bread,
Then Potamus Hippo will have the snack he loves most!"

"When he treads on the corn he will crush it all up
And we can bake bread from the flour.
We'll cut it in slices and add a few spices
And have excellent toast in an hour."

"We'll get plenty of peanuts to spread in his way,
We'll add berries and cherries and plums.
Potamus will squash it all into peanut butter and jelly,
And we'll spread it on toast with our thumbs."

While everyone rushed to get everything done,
Young Potamus roamed through the wood.
He stomped on the peanuts, berries and plums
Just as the wise Lion said he would.

When Potamus Hippo stomped back up the road
A wonderful sight met his eyes.
For there was a pile of his favorite food,
And it almost reached up to the sky!

Oh, what a feast young Potamus had,
He got peanut butter all over his nose!
Now he never stomps or makes his friends sad,
He only walks on his tippy-toes!